OSCAR

written by Kailyne R. Waters

•

illustrated by Pilar Lama

CHAPTER ONE

One sunny morning, a shopping cart woke up. He knew he woke up because he suddenly saw and heard things. Things he had never seen or heard before. He saw packages of food and bundles that burped. He heard horns that beeped and birds that sang.

I'M ALIVE!

The shopping cart liked the feeling of feeling alive. He discovered that he liked when his frame steadied the walk of an older person, or when a child fit snugly inside his basket. These moments gave him the inkling that maybe, just maybe, waking up meant *something*.

The shopping cart had other feelings too. Feelings that made him uneasy. He felt the constant tug against his frame. Those hands hurt! So much so that he attempted all sorts of ways to take a break. **CAMOUFLAGE!** as he blended in behind the garden plants. **FROZEN STATUE!** as he guided his wheels to an eerie standstill.

But those hands always found him and yanked him back. Finally, out of exhaustion, he rebelled. As a set of bony fingers tightened their grip around him, he pulled away with all his might and his back wheel **SNAPPED.**

A broken wheel was a huge problem for this shopping cart. For all shopping carts really, except they weren't awake to know it. He knew that broken meant done. Kaput.

Broken meant **CHUCK.**

Choukichi was his given name, but most knew him as Chuck. He drove the truck that barreled into the store lot and took away the carts that didn't roll anymore. Chuck the Junkyard Collector was good at his job. Too good. He was strong from lifting heaps of metal above his head for a living and could snatch a cart with just the tips of his fingers. He was light on his feet for such a tough guy. There wasn't anything he couldn't catch.

The shopping cart was so afraid of Chuck that he tried to hide next to a pair of newer carts. **DRAT!** He stuck out way too much because he wasn't sparkling like them.

If I can get shiny, I might stand a chance. The shopping cart bolted, flying past the produce stand as the sprinklers turned on. He was tickled by the cool water. *Ahhh…Refreshing!* He dried off in the sun and gleamed a bright silver. *Yes, this will do just fine,* he thought.

He was so HAPPY that he twirled and danced until…

THUD! He felt his broken wheel drag across the parking lot. The happiness left him. He didn't sound like everyone else, he sounded broken. *CHUCK.*

I have to hide! The shopping cart remembered the old, rusty dumpster at the side of the store. He clunked over and slid behind it. He heard a long, raspy sigh. *"Hiding won't help."* The shopping cart turned to the dumpster. *"Were you talking to me?"*

"Do you see anyone else?" replied Dumpster. *"Uh, no,"* the shopping cart stammered. *"Well then,"* Dumpster answered.

The shopping cart was so relieved to find someone to talk to that his words spilled out, *"You're alive like me! Except I'm broken. Why won't hiding help?"*

Dumpster paused and then replied, *"Occasionally we should be found."*

"But I'll be taken away. Taken to that place," the shopping cart pleaded.

Dumpster spoke, *"Ah yes, the graveyard for things. It is an interesting place. Many things that go need to be there. But sometimes, well, sometimes, things go that shouldn't."*

"Like me!" the shopping cart screamed. *"I have more to do. I have purpose."*

"Purpose?" asked Dumpster. The shopping cart explained, *"It's a word that means..."* *"I know what it means,"* Dumpster interrupted: *"The question is, do you?"*

"It means what you do when you're awake, alive like us. What's your purpose?" the shopping cart earnestly asked.

"I get filled, then picked up, emptied, and put down," Dumpster stated.

"Do you like being up there, way in the sky?" the shopping cart asked.

"I do, but it's not for you. In fact, when you get to the Vulture..."

"The Vulture?" the shopping cart's voice cracked.

"Yes, the graveyard has a very nasty Vulture that will lift you high in the air..." The shopping cart's cage rattled in fear. *"I am telling you this not to frighten you, but to assist you. You must escape."*

"But Chuck!" the shopping cart blurted out.

"Chuck isn't all that he seems," Dumpster replied calmly.

It was too much for the shopping cart. *"I'm broken, maybe my purpose is over,"* he said, dejected.

Then Dumpster spoke again, *"Or maybe it's just beginning..."*

Before he could ask what Dumpster meant, Chuck's truck **ROARED** into the parking lot. Chuck jumped out and landed with a confident thump. The shopping cart tucked his frame tight alongside the building, lurking in Dumpster's shadow. Chuck's eyes narrowed as he surveyed the lot. *"I'm gonna make a run for it!"* the shopping cart blurted.

"He'll see you!" Dumpster warned.

"Not if I'm careful! You want to come with me? You have wheels on the bottom. I saw them!"

"Not my time," Dumpster punctuated his sentence with a big yawn.

Maybe Dumpster was right about being caught, but maybe he was afraid too. *Why else would he have wheels if he wasn't supposed to move?*

The shopping cart decided to risk it and took off. *"Bon voyage, Purpose!"* Dumpster called. *That's not my name.* Not that the shopping cart knew his name, he just knew that it wasn't Purpose. His wheels spun faster and faster. It wasn't fast enough. It was hardly a race. Chuck snagged him, lifting him over his head, then tossing him into the truck. **CLUNK!** The shopping cart's steel bars **SHOOK!**

The truck rocketed through town leaving behind the only home he ever knew. He tried to calm himself by looking at the clouds, watching them swirl and change shapes, and listening for the whistles and peeps of the birds.

When the truck stopped at a schoolyard, the shopping cart saw a little boy standing alone. He could just make out the name on the back of his football jersey, etched with permanent marker.
CHARLIE.

♦ CHAPTER TWO

Charlie was distinct in many ways. Not just because he wore leg braces from an illness that hurt him when he was a baby, but mostly because no matter how much the other kids ignored him, the kinder he became. From his place on the bench, he would cheer them on with a big smile as they sped past him. Most kids would give up. But not Charlie. He cheered all the harder the next time. It wasn't that his classmates were intentionally mean, although some were. It was more that they just didn't think to include him. Charlie wanted so badly to play with them, especially the football kids. He loved wearing his father's jersey. Charlie didn't care that the only place it wasn't faded was where he had written his own name on it in art class. Charlie's favorite class.

And the art teacher, **MISS ELLA**, was his favorite teacher. She was the kind of teacher that every kid wanted. She could take anything that was thrown away and make it special. She dressed in bright colors with polka dots and stripes and encouraged the students to see beyond what was in front of them.

She inspired Charlie and his classmates to try new things and to embrace their artwork no matter if the paint ran off the page or dried before they could fix a stroke or line that got away from them. She showed Charlie how to make little birds out of old wire. At first, he only saw how rusty the wire looked and how bent and out of shape it was. But with Miss Ella's guidance, it turned into more. It was as if the birds were there all along just waiting to be found.

Charlie enjoyed making them, but the part he loved most was giving them away. The only classmates he didn't give birds to were the football kids. They were a few grades older and way cooler. On most days Charlie was fine being by himself and using his **IMAGINATION**.

Even though it was a big word, Charlie wasn't afraid of it. He learned very early on how wonderful a word imagination could be, and about the wonderful places he could visit, if he were just willing to try.

It was his mom who inspired Charlie to be creative. Together they would play pirates who couldn't swim, so they sailed on the carpet; or angels with broken wings who built propellers. It was easy to play these games because his mom had a grab bag of what she called leftovers.

She cleaned houses for a living, mostly those of people who had passed on, and she was permitted to take things with her. Every room of their home was decorated with forts and castles, or dungeons and rocket launch pads, made from the trinkets she collected. Even though she did her best to make experiences special for Charlie, he knew she was worried about him because the wrinkle above her nose didn't go away.

She said if he wanted to live his best happy life, he would have to find a way around the brokenness and, in fact, sometimes the broken parts are really the best parts of all. She would be there if he needed him, but it was up to him to say so. Just that morning he had said as much when he reminded her about the football kids and recess. She reminded him that the only reason anything was a **PROBLEM** was because the **SOLUTION** had fallen asleep.

It didn't feel like sleep to Charlie, it felt more like a deep freeze as he shifted his weight on the bench. Right before recess, Miss Ella reminded her students that today was her last day. She was officially retiring. Charlie knew she didn't want to because her voice trailed off and her smile was a sad one.

Miss Ella looked out her classroom window as Chuck's noisy truck came to a stop at the light. She gave a wave to her former student, and Chuck gave a hearty wave back. She saw the shopping cart too and noticed that he was looking at Charlie. The fact that he seemed to be looking didn't surprise her. In her years crafting art from objects, she came to believe that some were alive...sometimes. And in their own way, these gadgets glowed with purpose.

The shopping cart watched Charlie from his perch on top of the junk pile. He felt a connection with the boy and a familiar feeling crept over him. The feeling he had at the grocery store when he woke up and realized that just maybe there was *something* else he was supposed to *do*, or even more so, *be*. This notion stayed with him as the truck moved away. It stayed with him **until...**

CHAPTER THREE

SCREECH! A tall shadow passed by, and he saw the **VULTURE**, just like Dumpster had described! The winds howled as the Vulture caught the scared shopping cart in her claws, lifting him high above the ground. He felt free and wondered if this is what Dumpster felt too, until he saw what was happening. He was being carried to a conveyor belt that disappeared into a dark hole. Chuck pulled a large lever that made the belt lurch forward. A desire rose in the shopping cart that rivaled his fear...

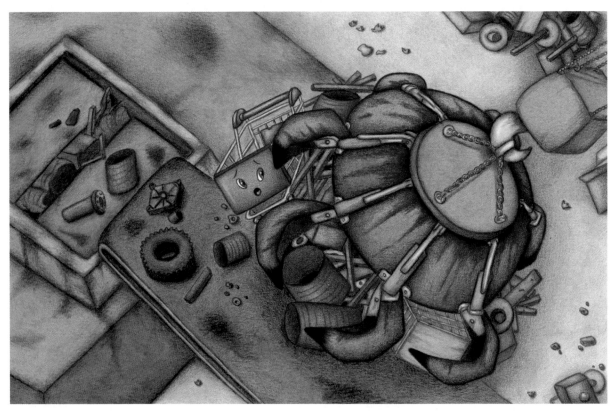

...DETERMINATION!

He was not going without a fight. And fight he did. Pulling, tugging, and straining with all his might. He couldn't believe it when he tumbled free hitting the ground with such force that his broken wheel righted itself! Not perfectly, but enough that he could move. He took off like a bullet. From behind him he could hear footsteps closing in. *Chuck!* But this time, he had a jump-start and a wheel that almost worked.

A train approached in the distance, gathering steam as it sped towards them. The shopping cart bounded for the clearing to get past its massive frame. *I won't make it!*

SUDDENLY, a swift shove from behind sent him flying!

Did Chuck just push me to safety? As the train blurred between them, he thought, *Dumpster was right, there IS more to Chuck!* When the train passed, he saw Chuck dancing! *He's like me!* The shopping cart danced too! He spun around, pausing and going, zigging, and zagging!

He stopped to ponder if he could be a dancing Junkyard Collector like Chuck. Or maybe an artist like the kids who played with chalk on the sidewalk, or a chef like the ones who stood in the grocery store handing out hot pizza bites.

He was entertained by these ideas then considered: *What is MY purpose?*

Maybe my purpose has to do with Charlie? With that in mind, the shopping cart turned to the horizon and set out to find him.

CHAPTER FOUR

The shopping cart arrived at the schoolyard and found Charlie watching the football kids play. He crept up behind him and gave Charlie a slight bump. Charlie looked at him and the shopping cart took this as an invitation and bumped him lightly again.

"Whoa! What a neat cart!" Charlie mused. He studied the shopping cart, sizing him up for an adventure. And he knew just what to do. His last art project was tying colorful ribbons together. By themselves they were just ribbons, but when tied together they formed MAGIC. They gave whoever held them the power to think brave thoughts, that's what Miss Ella said. He pulled the ribbons out of his pocket and tied them to the shopping cart.

Dropping his crutches into the cart, Charlie hoisted himself in. He raised one crutch and called *"Charge, Oscar! Charge!"*

Oscar? Is that my name? My name is Oscar! And what a good name too! Oscar felt as colorful as the ribbons.

Charlie cried again, *"**Charge, Oscar! CHARGE!**"* And to Charlie's delight, Oscar did!

The kids watched as Charlie soared past them, and soon they followed. A few grabbed Oscar, but he didn't mind. He was focused on Charlie's commanding grip, his eyes lit like tiny flames as he led Oscar into an imaginary battlefield teeming with unslain dragons. From his throne, Charlie saw his classmates, even the older and way cooler ones, following his lead. **He gripped Oscar tighter and forged on!**

RIIINNNNG! All at once the playing stopped, and the kids raced away from Charlie, ending the best recess there ever was. Still beaming, Charlie gathered his crutches and jumped out of the cart. Then he saw the students lining up by Miss Ella, who had placed a big, floppy crepe paper flower behind her ear. Head hanging low, he walked over to his place in line, leaving Oscar behind.

HURT. It was an uncomfortable emotion that grew Oscar's sadness inside. He watched as each student filed past Miss Ella, hugging her goodbye. When it was Charlie's turn, he gave her a hug and the prettiest bird he ever made. *Charlie is hurting too*, Oscar realized. Discouraged and unable to think of what to do, he turned away.

A moment later, there was a soft touch from a gentle hand. Turning back, he saw Miss Ella. She had an idea when she saw Charlie full of life, sailing by in the shopping cart, the wheels flying underneath him. She knew that Charlie's mom couldn't afford to buy a wheelchair even with the assistance she received from the hospital. *This will be my gift to them*, she thought. Leaning close to Oscar, she whispered *"Would you like to help me build a wheelchair for Charlie?"*

Oscar's heart soared. He felt connected to her, the same way he felt connected to Charlie.

Maybe this is what friendship feels like? As they traveled down the street to Miss Ella's home, a sensation he would come to know as hope, welled up inside.

CHAPTER FIVE

Oscar was amazed when Miss Ella opened her garage door. It looked like a lush garden full of fresh shapes and sizes. A few were practical things like clock radios and cooking pots, and others not as practical like an ironing board that growled when it snapped in place, and an electric can opener that oinked when it turned.

They spent the day gathering trinkets, and the odds and ends of colorful wheels and speedy motors. He liked spending time with Miss Ella. At night she would tinker away, whistling as she worked. It reminded Oscar of cheerful birds and made him nostalgic for sounds he left long ago.

He missed his home but was happy here too. Oscar knew that together he and Miss Ella were building something for Charlie. She would talk to him like friends do. ***"What do you think of this one?"*** she'd say, holding up a bike tire. She didn't wait for Oscar to answer, but he didn't mind. He was thrilled that Miss Ella trusted him and was excited to be a part of her purpose. But it would seem no matter how hard she worked, the chairs she made would not. Oscar could sense that her impatience was growing. Finally, one night, she threw up her hands and walked out, shutting off the light and leaving Oscar without another word.

Charlie and his mom had eaten dinner by candlelight so many nights in a row that Charlie could barely find his plate with the flicker of the only remaining nub of candle.

His mom tried to make a game of it, but Charlie could see through that and wished she would stop treating him like a baby.

He picked at the thread on his jersey because he knew it annoyed her. It worked too. She scolded him and told him to stop tugging or it might unravel for good. *"What difference does it make?"* Charlie said. *"I'll never be a football player like Dad."*

His mom looked at him in a new serious way, more serious than any wrinkle above her nose. *"Charlie, your father was a great football player because he understood there was much more to the game than running. You are more than that too. More than that jersey, the wire birds, or even my son. You have your own life and a way to make it so."* Charlie thought about it, not entirely convinced, but not entirely against what she was saying either. *"I have an idea,"* she said. *"Why don't we visit Miss Ella? I miss her too."* Charlie perked up a little at that and together they planned their trip.

Oscar sat in the darkness of the garage and worried. *What's to become of me?* He remembered his friend Dumpster and could almost hear him telling Oscar to sit still. But he didn't want to sit still. *I must get her attention,* he concluded. He started to twirl and spin, faster and faster until he bumped into boxes that teetered and finally **CRASHED** to the ground. Oscar froze.

A light came on and Miss Ella opened the door. Something caught her eye. Oscar followed her gaze: Charlie's wire bird had fallen to the floor.

She picked it up and seemed sad, but then her eyes lit with shimmering flames. *Charlie! My students! I can't give up!* But she couldn't do it alone. *Alone.* How many times did she remind her students that it was noble to ask for help? She needed help and she knew exactly who to ask!

CHAPTER SIX

The next morning Oscar heard Chuck's truck in the driveway! He felt a slight tremor in his frame. ***Did Chuck truly save me at the graveyard?*** Miss Ella invited Chuck into the garage and showed him the wheelchair. He gave a friendly tap to Oscar as he passed by, ***"Glad you made it through, buddy!"*** Oscar beamed, totally giddy with delight. He had another **NEW FRIEND** to admire!

Chuck and Miss Ella set to work on making the wheels roll right, and before long, they had done just that! Miss Ella thanked Chuck by offering him tea. They sat together on milk crates turned upside down and dunked large cookies into their teacups. Amused, Oscar watched Chuck dip his cookie, his fingers as light as his toes. A short while later, Chuck thanked Miss Ella and was out the door with a wave.

Just in time too! Charlie and his mom had arrived for their visit.
Miss Ella could hardly contain her joy. Charlie vaulted towards the
wheelchair and his mom's face flooded with gratitude. *"Oh, Miss Ella,
it's wonderful!"* she exclaimed. Miss Ella beamed. The three celebrated
by taking turns in the driveway riding the wheelchair up and back!

Oscar was **OVERJOYED! THIS** was happiness!

Later that evening when all was still, Oscar thought more about his life. Charlie had his wheelchair, and he wondered if his purpose might be over. He fell into a deep sleep and had a dream…

The sun streaked across the sky like lightning bolts. He heard the loud **SCREECHING** thunder of the Vulture. Standing on the outside and looking in, he noticed something. It wasn't actually a vulture. It was mechanical, like the objects that Miss Ella builds. The parts were going in as one thing and coming out as another. That's not too scary, Oscar thought. Just then a booming voice he recognized as Dumpster spoke: *"Welcome back, Purpose."* Instantly Oscar was at his old home, the grocery store. He saw himself wedged in the line of shopping carts, motionless.

Oscar woke feeling a bit uneasy, so he was grateful when Miss Ella took him to town with her. She had decided to share her colorful art displays with local businesses and had stacked them proudly in Oscar's carriage. But when they stopped at the grocery store, Oscar remembered his dream.

The old, rusty Dumpster stood against the wall, and the bright, shiny carts were neat in a row. Everything was the same. Everything except him. While Miss Ella talked to the store owner, Oscar decided to pay Dumpster a visit to discuss his new life, but a flash of motion caught his attention.

He saw a baby in a shopping cart, rolling away! With no regard for his own safety, Oscar zoomed towards it. Throwing his body against the runaway cart and turning his special wheel on its side, he stopped it! *The baby was safe!* Oscar felt the warmth that made him who he was. *AHHH! WONDERFUL!* Until...

"Look out, Purpose!" cried Dumpster.

SMASH!!! A bus roaring by knocked Oscar off the ground and sent him somersaulting across the street and down into tangles and tangles of brush. His cage rattled a branch and his special wheel flew off and landed far away. He was stunned, quiet, except for his beating frame as he teetered on three wheels. *Where am I?* A wave of deep hopelessness overcame him. *How can I possibly be of use to anyone now?*

He heard the crinkle of leaves under footsteps and a whistle. Not just any whistle. *Miss Ella!* She was carrying his wheel. As she gently knelt beside Oscar, relief swept over him. She repaired his brokenness by giving him his wheel back and replacing the bent washer with a new one.

Just then a Mother Bird's SQUAWKS and CHATTERS were heard above him. *What was making her create such a commotion?* Miss Ella saw it first as her gaze fell upon Oscar's carriage.

A nest with three fragile, unhatched eggs had fallen in during his tumble. Miss Ella smiled a sweet smile, gave a gentle tap to Oscar's frame, and then let go, walking back into the tangles of brush without him.

As she disappeared from his sight, Oscar thought, *no, please don't leave me! Not here, not now.* The **CHIRPS** of the Mother Bird called him back. She carefully pecked away and removed a colorful ribbon tied to Oscar and gently weaved it into her nest. He felt exceptionally small, but a familiar feeling stirred in him, a feeling of being useful. He knew, deep inside he knew, it was right to stay. It was right to be a home for a Mother Bird and her family. *Dumpster would be proud of me,* he thought, trying to comfort himself so far away from any place or anyone he had ever known.

CHAPTER SEVEN

Oscar grew to enjoy his situation and after a time the birds were ready to hatch. Out they popped, first one then the other, except the last one didn't budge. The Mother Bird pecked and worried, and pecked a little more, but the egg would not open. Oscar rocked back and forth offering a lullaby. His repaired, special wheel now made a funny, squeaky noise. This embarrassed Oscar a little, but he pressed on with it, determined to help.

Finally, the baby hatched, and unlike her brothers, her eyes were wide open!

Charlie's eyes were wide open too as he focused on the limb just above his head. He grabbed on to it and yanked himself up. Something had changed in Charlie. He had taken to climbing trees, not way up in the tall branches, but the lower ones.

He never wanted to before. He used to feel embarrassed that the other kids his age could climb up high, he didn't seem to mind much now. He rested on a branch and watched his mom below. She was fretting over his wheelchair. Something was broken. And this time it was beyond what she could do to repair it. He assured her that he would be okay. And he meant it. Even without the use of his chair, he was content. His mom called him down and together they headed to the repair shop. With Charlie's hand linked with his mom's he reminded her what she always said:

"Sometimes the broken parts of ourselves are our best parts of all."

Soon after Charlie and his mom left the shop with the part in hand and bad news from the owner that they couldn't fix what was broken. Magically it was then they passed by one of Miss Ella's art pieces. Charlie noticed it right away, but it took an extra tug of his mom's hand before she turned to notice too. It was a flattened bicycle wheel molded into a window frame. The spokes were straightened to look like windowpanes. One of Charlie's wire birds sat on a spoke.

"Whoa! That's so cool!" Charlie announced. *"Miss Ella chose my bird!"* Just then, a sense of relief flooded Charlie's mom.

Of course! Miss Ella would know what to do!

Miss Ella was about to close her garage for the day when she saw them waving to her. Charlie's mom explained about the chair and told Miss Ella if anyone could help it would be her.

Together they tinkered with Charlie's chair. Everything came down to one bent washer. Miss Ella blinked in disbelief. ***It's not possible,*** she thought. But it was more than possible, it was marvelous. She found the bent washer she had taken from Oscar and placed it up to the rod in Charlie's chair, and it fit...**perfectly!**

Good fortune had landed with Oscar too. He was part of a new and exciting adventure! As the days went by, Oscar provided a haven for the Mother Bird and her fledglings. He offered the occasional squeaky, but gentle rocking back and forth whenever the littlest and most unique baby tried to keep up with her brothers. But, for the most part, he did no rolling at all.

🐦 CHAPTER EIGHT

The summer passed, and Oscar felt the tickle of leaves on his wheels. As they had begun to fly from the trees, so did the birds from their nest. Baby number one and two landed gently onto a branch next to their mother. After a moment, number three joined them, skidding to an awkward stop. The Mother Bird called out to them. The first two responded with a soft whistle, but the last let out a rumbly, little squeak not unlike Oscar's wheel, that sounded remarkably like *I love you.*

Love, Oscar observed. ***Yes, it is love.*** His heart as warm as the sun.

The Mother Bird tucked her special little one under her wing, snuggling her like a soft blanket. Oscar looked at the Mother Bird and her offspring perched high in the tree and knew it was time to go. The months there taught him that he had value no matter if he could roll or not. What mattered most is that he was there for others. He now knew wherever he landed, he would be okay, and it would be enough. Saying goodbye to his friends, Oscar practically skipped as he wheeled away.

Now Charlie's wheels were supercharged. Miss Ella had given them a little boost, although Charlie's mom thought it might be cheating, Charlie didn't think so, and his classmates didn't seem to mind either.

Standing at the schoolyard, Miss Ella thought about all the students she had taught, all the hugs she had given, and the stories she had told. She was a little sad, but she was surprised that overall, she was happy. She enjoyed seeing the students and was especially pleased to see Charlie finally playing what he loved most: football. She had hoped that he would still find time for art too, and she was delighted to learn that it was Charlie who had suggested that they wear colorful ribbons around their waists for flag football. His ribbons were tied to the back of his chair, glistening in the sun like magic. Charlie's mom joined Miss Ella and together they celebrated Charlie being Charlie.

Oscar strode through the archway of trees that opened to a golden path. He rode up the hill and landed on street level. He knew exactly where he wanted to go. He reached the school and there it all was, just as he had hoped.

Oscar wasn't sure how, but he knew that *his* part of the story mattered here. He especially knew it when he saw Miss Ella smile at him like a friend greeting a friend. Charlie stopped and gave a wave, *"Hey, Oscar!"*

No one was more surprised than Oscar when Charlie headed over and clasped the old strand of ribbon dangling from his frame and weaved a brand new one into it. To Oscar it felt like he was receiving a medal of honor. He sensed the rush of the best feelings ever take over. Then in a flash, Charlie dashed away to join his friends.

Oscar stayed for a while, basking in the warmth. He wondered what it would be like to be remembered by Charlie, Miss Ella, the Mother Bird and her babies, and even Chuck. Would they think of him and his squeaky wheel whenever they saw or heard something different or broken? Perhaps they would believe that was the best part, the part where bravery came from. He hoped his wheels would live on in their hearts. Maybe that's really all he could do in life, be kind and keep rolling through the rough patches, being himself, wherever the journey brought him.

Oscar sighed. *Was it too much to hope for? Nah.* He saw it now, and before he saw it, he had discovered it deep inside. He took a last look at his friends and then turned towards the horizon. There were many more places to see, many more people to help. All he ever wanted was to be the shopping cart that made a difference, and at last he could. He finally got it. Deep inside of him was the best home of all. A home that had...

"*PURPOSE!*"

Oscar spun around. It was Dumpster and he was being hauled off, not by Chuck, but by a monster tow truck, sparks flying as his metal scraped along the pavement.

"*PURPOSE!!!*" Dumpster shouted again. Oscar didn't hesitate a moment longer, his wheels spun as they leapt into action, the ribbons sparkling like streaks of dazzled lightning.

"*On my way!*"

The author:
Kailyne Waters is a writer and filmmaker who made a shopping cart come to life in the short film: The Go Cart. The animated tale screened at festivals around the world and won cool awards. She's created content for community organizations to help teens, houseless people, and persons with disabilities. Kailyne enjoys dreaming up stories, her local library (where she was a proud part of the mighty circulation team) and wearing fuzzy socks. This is her first children's book.

The illustrator:
Pilar Lama was born and raised in Madrid, Spain. With a specialized education in children's illustration, she likes to use several different techniques, including pencil, watercolor, acrylic, gouache, ink and digital. Pilar is an open minded, outgoing, kind and happy hard-worker. She is a very imaginative person and never stops dreaming up new ideas. Her drawings are characterized by a wide range of bright colors that show the passion she brings to each of her projects. Pilar is represented by WendyLynn & Co.

ISBN # 978-0-578-28677-8